www.tredition.de

VALERIE MILIČEVIĆ

***

LIFE'S A LAUGH

Memoirs

www.tredition.de

© 2021 Valerie Miličević

Verlag und Druck:
tredition GmbH, Halenreie 40-44, 22359 Hamburg

ISBN
Paperback: 978-3-347-18191-5
Hardcover: 978-3-347-18192-2
e-Book: 978-3-347-18193-9

Foreword

This story was told to me backwards, starting with the good old London days, hopping to Johannesburg, then on to more recent times and lastly to where life began in earnest for Valerie Griffin Miličević in Scotland.

I had heard some of the 'good uns' over the years, nearly always accompanied by red wine, a few smokes and belly laughs. Fasten your seatbelts, here we go!

Life's a Laugh

"A man should be tall enough to keep his head in the clouds and his feet planted firmly on the ground" –

Abraham Lincoln

Dedicated to Ivor, Gone but not Forgotten

Part 1 Bonnie Scotland and the School Years

I guess you could say that the rot set in at primary school in Scotland. I was a rebel even then. I remember playing truant and raiding Mrs McFee's crab apple tree and on another occasion, leading an expedition down the neighbouring quarry, all of us children tied together with ropes.

At St John and Columba's high school I was a complete duffer at maths.

One day I asked my dad to help me with my algebra homework. My dad was a bit of a maths fundi which I could never understand as, times being tight, he left school at fourteen years to join Chatham dockyard, transferring to Rosyth dockyard when I was two and a half.

"Griffin (no respect!) Come here!" Oh heck, what has my dad done now! Approaching his desk, he said, "What is the meaning of this!". "Well Sir, it was a bit diff diff. ." "Oh, I know YOU didn't do it! I want to meet your father". "My f f father Sir?" "Yes, I want to know how your father solved my algebraic equation in six lines when it's taken me the whole bloody blackboard!"

Being a myope, I was seated in the front row of the maths class. Rarely wearing my specs, I couldn't see much of what was going on. Gradually, I moved back, a few rows at a time until I was seated in the back row. A sharp shifty to the right saw me out the door and sitting quietly in a corner of the art room next door, gazing in awe at all the artistic endeavours going on around me. After a few weeks the art master, Mr C, said if I was going to sit there for hours, I might as well join in. And so, it was that I got my Higher Art! Not that I went to Art College. I couldn't wait to get out into the big wide world!

One week we were due to have an art inspection. The day before I suggested we play a joke on Mr. C. We would redecorate the art room. Each of us had to bring in certain articles from home, a wig, beanies, ribbons, streamers, toilet rolls and an onion and carrot. We were to arrive very early and set to work. The result was priceless! Then we scarpered to await Mr C's arrival.

Mouth agape, specs falling down his nose, he couldn't believe his eyes! But we felt so sorry for him that we couldn't bear it any longer and emerged from our hiding places. We soon had the art system room restored to its original pristine condition, but I'm quite sure Mr. C regretted ever inviting me to join his art class! But it had made school life so much more interesting and fun. Soon after I was made Head Girl, to teach me to set an example to others. Thus, ended all my shenanigans!

Awaiting the results of my Higher Leaving Certificate, my dad suggested I sit the Civil Service exam. When the results were released, I had scored good marks and was thus allowed to choose which ministry I preferred and being a people person, I opted for the Ministry of Labour. After three month's training in my home town, I was transferred to London, to the Hotel and Catering employment exchange in Tin Pan Alley.

Part 2 London

Our flat was in Tachbrook Street.
We had a basement flat with grape vines growing in the
garden, puny little grapes as no sun got in, but imagine,
grape vines in the middle of London! I shared seven flats
in London days and they all had one thing in common...
Irish landlords!

My landlords were all great. One took such a shine to
us that he didn't come to collect the rent for months on end.
Then he'd rock up for coffee and present us with an astronomical bill for rent, the water and lights, telephone etc! I
told him he was nuts as we could have scarpered!

My favourite memory

My first boyfriend after my transfer to London was a
Scottie from Edinburgh, Ivor. He was doing his National
Service as a military policeman at Kensington Barracks
and I was living in a nearby civil service hostel. Not able
to invite each other in for coffee, we spent our evenings
walking the streets of London, having a cuddle behind the
Albert Hall.

One evening we decided for a lark and a bit of variety to
go skinny dipping in the Serpentine. It being after hours,
Hyde Park was all locked up but with the aid of an up-
turned waste paper basket and his strong arms, he hoisted
me over. We had the whole of Hyde Park to do our cnoo-
dling! I can't remember skinny dipping though so for the
sake of authenticity, safer to say we didn't! I said that if we

got caught, he wearing his uniform could say he was just rescuing a damsel in distress! But it had all been such fun.

After his demob he returned to Edinburgh. We corresponded a few times and he wrote me a lovely letter to say that if I did get the flat, I was planning to do, to send him my address and he would pay me a flying visit some weekend. He found Edinburgh like a morgue after London, hated his job as a compositor, felt the Police was his vocation and intended to apply to the Colonial Police.

Well sadly we lost touch as one does in London and to this day I can't understand why. Perhaps my reply went astray but it has been my biggest regret. They just don't make them like that anymore! Tall, manly, protective and great fun.

The short-sighted lunatic

At one time, Norma and I shared a basement flat in Holland Road W 14. We had one half of the basement, Miss S, our Irish landlady, the other, separated by a heavy door. She came to us one day and told us to expect a plumber early the next morning, coming to fix a leaky tap in bathroom and said to let him in.

At some ungodly hour the doorbell rings and Norma dashes out, clad only in a skimpy nighty. Screams ensue and I thought it was a ruse to get me up so I stayed put in bed. However, the screams got more frantic, so I dashed to the kitchen to find Norma being flung around by some crazed bespectacled youth. Grabbing his specs, I threw them across the floor and together we managed to shove him out the door. So strong was he that the door came off its hinges!

Miss S meantime, too scared to investigate, dashed upstairs and grabbed two Irish tenants for moral support. By the time they arrived, oke* had fled. The cops duly arrived, thinking it a huge joke, despite our bruises and scratches. It appears oke was an escaped lunatic from Springfield Asylum! He had turned himself in, no doubt unable to find his way home without his specs!

*Afrikaans: guy

The Princess and... the hot water bottle

I never used to strip my bed, just hauling covers up before dashing off to work. In the cold winter months, I used to put a hot water bottle at my feet. One night the bed collapsed with me in it.

On investigation, I found a forgotten hot water bottle had burst, rotting the bedpost at the bottom of the bed. So incensed was Miss S, that she made me sleep for months with the bed propped up on bricks!

At least the Tokoloshe* didn't get me!

* South Africa; a mischievous and evil spirit. According to legend, the only way to keep the Tokoloshe away at night is to put a brick beneath each leg of one's bed.

Royal Burgundy

To make extra cash, I used to head a team of six girls, prepared to help out at various functions around the City. At one such event I was the wine waitress at the Savoy hotel's main table at which Princess Alexandra was the guest of honour. Preparing to pour her wine, for some inexplicable reason I tripped, sloshing red wine down her cleavage and all down the front of her red velvet dress.

Goodbye sweet job, I groaned, but undaunted the gracious lady said plenty more where this came from, exiting to her dressing room and reappearing moments later in an identical outfit. My Supervisor was none the wiser.

She's been my favourite royal ever since!

Hollow legs

On transfer to London, I was housed in a Civil Service hostel in Hyde Park Gate. Working at a function for the Polish Harvest Festival at the Festival Hall, I was in charge of the coffee machine.

Time and again a certain Pole swayed towards me for coffee until I got pissed off and said "You're drunk and if you ask me for one more cup of coffee, I'll tip the pot over your head!" Next day one of the hostel residents came to me and said there were two blokes downstairs wanting to talk to me. "What do they look like?" I asked. "Never mind what they look like, you should see the limo!"

So, intrigued I go down to be confronted by dronkie* and his mate, come to ask Norma and I out to dinner. "By the way, I'm not a drunk, just have two wooden legs, courtesy of a motor bike accident in Scotland!" Well to say how terrible I felt would be putting it mildly!

We duly went out to dinner, had a great time and went back to their apartment for coffee. We find the walls of the apartment are papered with dozens of autographed photos taken with the various celebrities they'd met in their travels around the globe as entertainers!

*Afrikaans: drunk person

The Scotch Marigold at Claridge's

Sitting in my office at the Ministry of Labour, I get a phone call from one of the managers at Claridge's, a posh 5 star, and the only London hotel where the Royal family stayed. He was looking for the services of a temporary kitchen hand for the busy summer season. Well always on the lookout for extra cash, I offered my services. "Oh no!", he said, "we only employ males here", so I put the phone down. Minutes later it rings again. "Did you just cut me off?" he asked. "By accident" I lied.

Anyway, before long I'd persuaded him to see me. A very elegant Italian in his seventies, we hit it off and I was taken on as a washer up. He wasn't at all happy to have me washing dishes though I said I didn't mind. A few weeks later he said he was putting me on Room Service. It seems they were having problems with the good-looking males being propositioned and as the customer is always right, he was having to fire them. So, for the next three seasons I was employed on Room Service, a cushy job and I could order my food from the guest menu...divine! One evening, arriving for duty I exited the lift and some cheeky Italian shoved a trolly behind my knees, sending me flying along the corridor, straight into the arms of the General Manager! Looking at me he said "Well, it has never happened at Claridge's before but there's always a first time!"

No-one propositioned me but they'd have met their match! Aristotle Onassis had a permanent suite on my floor but he rarely pitched so I could not get propositioned by a shipping magnate!

Staying with Claridge's, a waiter reported that the best china monogrammed cups, saucers and plates were disappearing at an alarming rate from the room of a certain American. Unable to accuse him without proof, on the day of his departure, when his luggage was piled up in the lobby, the floor Manager instructed two porters to take it upstairs and throw it down, not once but 6 times!

I imagine the look on the Yank's face when he got home and opened his bags to find smashed crockery all over!

A wealthy French guest told the General Manager that he had left his watch behind in Paris and could he possibly spare one of the staff to fly there first class, at his expense, to fetch it. Delighted to get a day off, a valet duly obliged and brought back said watch, not a bejewelled Rolex as expected but a cheap affair which could be purchased locally at next to nothing and saving the airfare. When the

General Manager pointed this out, he said he had had it for years and was very attached to it! So many nutters around!

At the time of this story, I was sharing a flat in Earls Court Road. I had a dark green bedspread which was too unwieldy to wash by hand so I took it to the launderette at the bottom of the road. An hour later, to my horror, pukey green dye started sloshing around the launderette floor and soon all the machines had shorted. What to do while waiting for the manageress and a technician?

So, I suggested an impromptu launderette party. I being the cause of the fracas, went next door to the café and purchased snacks and cold drinks, someone produced the music, someone else beers and wine and before long our party was in full swing, Bemused passers-by joined in. The racket could have woken the dead! Needless to say, I had to dump offending cover and buy a new one, making sure it wasn't pukey green!

What a difference a ' k ' makes

Working at Claridge's, I met and went out with the Danish head of banqueting, Jorn (Johnny) from Odense (where Hans Christian Anderson was born). He was travelling the globe learning languages with the view of opening his own restaurant in the Tivoli Gardens, Copenhagen. After perfecting his English, he moved to Germany, working and living in at the Four Seasons in Hamburg. He invited me for a holiday and booked me into a nearby B and B. After dinner one evening, he dropped me off at my B and B in the wee small hours.

Finding the security gates, behind which sat an impassive night watchman, I looked in my bag for my keys but found I'd left them in my room. What to do? The only German I knew, apart from ich liebe dich which didn't seem appropriate, was, for some unknown reason, ich habe einen Schlüssel. Deciding to practice my German on impassive, "ich habe einen Schlüssel, ich habe einen Schlüssel, ich habe einen Schlüssel" I informed him but impassive remained just that.

Eventually the rumpus attracted the attention of the night manager who came down looking livid and a bit dishevelled. Oops I thought, I've disturbed something strategic here, noting shirt tail hanging out and hair awry! "Ich habe einen Schlüssel" I continued and in a broad Pommie accent he shouted, "Well if you've got a bloody key, why don't you bloody well come in!"

I should, of course, have said ich habe KEINEN Schlüssel! Well Johnny soon got me into a much nicer B and B, the owner of which had a young school going son. Having nothing better to do, I took him under my wing and taught him some basic English words. His Dad was so pleased that on my departure, he presented me with a bottle of Brandy!

Johnny Danish later proposed by letter but in such a roundabout way. He asked me if I intended to stay single, bit dull I should think! As for me, he wrote, I have to get married next year before my 30th birthday or get the peppermill. It is considered as a shame, any suggestions? Well, what do you think of that!

Was he expecting ME to propose! Anyway, he wasn't for me, bit too ambitious, concerned with wealth and his appearance, never met a bloke with so many clothes, suits, velvet smoking jackets etc. Of course, he did need a lot of them for his job. Then the travelling when I had a steady job in London which I loved (not to mention a certain lovely guy I'd met from Belfast who was living in South Africa but on a year's visit to London. He was a commercial artist).

I think I was very fickle in those days!

Fifty pounds

For a time, I had an evening job at the Connaught Rooms as a cloakroom attendant, banqueting rooms for Mason's dos. I earned a very basic salary plus tips which had to be pooled, our stingy supervisor claiming that biggest portion. She used to follow us around all over the place making sure we didn't pocket any tips!

One evening a very elegant lady approached me and said that if I guarded her mink with my life, she would see me right afterwards. I was to meet her in the ladies after the function. So pleased was she to find her precious mink all safe and sound, she gave me fifty pounds with strict instructions not to let hawk eyes get her greasy paws on it. But imagine, fifty pounds, a fortune in those days!

Funnies from my Ministry of Labour Days

A young woman comes in a seeking a job as a live-in chambermaid. "Are you prepared to share a room?" I asked. "Oi don't moined sharing a room, as long as it's with the chef and not another blerry chambermaid!"

The catering manager of the London Zoo rings up for some staff. Now it was quite common in those days to ask if employers would consider Irish or West Indians (neither of whom had a reputation for staying put; it would be considered racist today) so I give him my party piece. "oi don't mind Oirish, I'm Oirish meself but don't send any blerry Scots along!" That put me firmly in my place!

Another time I'm alone in the office, the others having gone to lunch. A hefty, rather scary looking oke comes in and hands me his CV containing very good references of his employment as a chef with HM Prisons. "I'd better tell you that I've just got out of jail after murdering my wife!"

Muchas gracias

Margie, one of my flatmates and I had booked a holiday in Palma De Mallorca. The day before departure, loaded down with new dress, shoes and patent leather handbag, I get off the tube and as the doors were closing, noticed my handbag containing passports, travellers' cheques, air tickets, repaired gold bracelet, prescription sun glasses, cash, flat keys and address book, sitting forlornly on the front seat.

Grabbing a porter, I asked him when next train to Baker Street was due. Lost property usually takes two days to be handed in. Well, I couldn't just stand there, so I boarded the next tube going to Baker Street.

Arriving at lost property the lady behind the counter asked me to describe bag and contents. She reappeared holding my bag and I found not a single thing missing, even the cash. "How on earth did it get to you so quickly?" "Well, you were lucky to be sitting in the front car with the driver."

Grabbing my bag, he handed it to a passing driver with instructions to hand it in to lost property pronto. "Well, he's saved my life so I'd like to give him a big reward, could you give me his name, address and phone number." "It's not the policy of British Rail to divulge that sort of information. Our staff are taught to be honest or risk losing their jobs."

Well, I was livid but there was nothing I could do! But such honesty in the middle of London in the rush hour! Unbelievable!

Brilliant being the operative word

Norma and I, living in Earls Court, used to frequent the OVC (Overseas Visitors Club). One Sunday we were listening to some jazz when approached by two very polite, well dressed young men who asked if they could join us. They said they were South Africans and invited us back to their apartment in St John's Wood (one of the most exclusive areas of London). Wow, that what a pad, plush white carpets, oil paintings everywhere and a baby grand, atop which was a large framed photo of their parents, an elegant couple dressed in full evening dress.

Where do two young guys get the money to afford such a pad, we mused. That evening they took us to a casino, not that we did any gambling, just sat there gazing in awe at the serious money changing hands! Waiters fawning all over them, one of them said "C'mon Sylvain, give us a song!" He obliged and what a great voice!

Years later, employed as Personnel Officer of National Trading Co. In Johannesburg, the Managing Director handed me a copy of a black and white mag called Comment and Opinion, containing up to date news of the day and current events. He asked me to read through it and let him know if I thought it would be beneficial to the staff, if so, he would order it and distribute it to the staff for free.

Browsing through, I come to the centre pages and there in glorious Technicolor was a picture of a very elegant lady holding a ginormous diamond, reputed to be the finest in the world and named the Premier Rose, after the part owner, Mrs Rose M.

She and her husband Joe were impoverished Belgian Jews, refugees who fled their country during the war, married in Turkey, before finally settling in Joburg where they opened up a diamond cutting works in De Villiers St. The diamond had been mined at the Cullinan in Pretoria and they had been given the task of cutting it.340 carats, it took six months and was worth R 3 million in 1978.

The story went on to say their two sons, Jacques managed the London operation, Sylvain the Joburg operation.

Yes, our two heroes from St John's Wood! Now I knew where they got their boodle from. If we'd known that, we would have hung in there!

Just so happens that they were the lads who helped us mop up after the Great Flood Disaster, a new experience for them I'm sure and a great story to tell their grandkids!

Posteriors saved for posterity

On holiday in Palma De Mallorca with mum and brother Dave, mum was lying down nursing a touch of sunburn, Dave checking out the talent on the beach. I decided to take my box brownie and try to get a pic of Palma Cathedral and its beautiful rose window. I soon had two cops chasing me, shouting hotel, hotel, hotel!

Why I thought, no cleavage showing, shorts yes but so did most other folk. To hell with them, I thought and led them a merry dance through the streets and in and out of shops. Arriving at a very narrow cobbled street, I thought aha they won't get their car down here! Arriving at the bottom, I was confronted by Palma Cathedral but how to take a picture in such a confined space. Looking across the way I see a soldier on duty at the gates of what looked like a castle.

Gesticulating with my camera and in broken Spanish, he got the message and let me in. Wow, I thought, but they've even laid out the red carpet for me! Just about to climb up onto a conveniently placed dais, with the banging of drums, blaring of trumpets and clashing of cymbals, in marched hundreds of troops. .it appears I was in the middle of the centenary celebrations for General Franco!

Shoving me into a sentry box, with instructions to shh, there I stood knees knocking, heart thumping for what seemed an eternity! Eventually, they moved to the inner sanctum to continue the ceremony. Well, I didn't come all this way for nothing so today I am the proud possessor of a black and white pic of Franco's rear end! Getting back to my hotel, my frantic mum was about to call the cops, and with my luck it would be the same two who had been chasing me all afternoon!

I went up to the front desk and asked what was wrong with my attire. Well in Spain, it is considered unseemly for ladies to appear in public with their arms uncovered. Can you believe that!? Anyway, that wasn't the end of the saga. For days I had my rescuer phoning the hotel to speak to me. "Who is this chap?" asked my mum. If only she knew!

I often wonder, given his reputation, what would have happened had I been.caught, left to rot in some Spanish dungeon, never to be heard of again, and what a loss that would have been to the world!

Ice-cream Sundae

While in Palma, I decided to visit a little boutique where I had espied a beautiful silk shirt in the window. Practising my little Spanish "Te quiero con todo mi Corazon" (I love you with all my heart), I proclaimed to the owner. "Una momento senorina" he said with a beaming smile, dashing out of the shop, leaving me with a few customers and an open till.

He returned ten minutes later bearing a ginormous ice cream sundae. I had, in the meantime, interested his customers in some shirts and leather handbags.

A sequel to this story, revisiting Palma four years later, I decided to see if the boutique was still in existence. "Te quiero con todo mi Corazon" I repeated. "Una momento" and off he dashed again. Amazing that after four years he still remembered me! I am truly unforgettable!

Dumb Waiter

Still living at the civil service hostel, I had a Saturday evening job at a restaurant in Fleet Street catering to the male editors of News of the World, just down the road. I was in charge of the service hatch, an antiquated affair operated by pulleys. I think it was called a Dumb Waiter.

I had to check orders were correct, no spillages, hand them to my boss, who delivered them to various tables. She used to pay my taxi fare home. One evening an editor, Roger, offered me a lift home saying it was on his way. We had a nice friendly chat with me telling him my life story, as is my wont.

Next day one of the girls handed me a copy of News of the World. Isn't this the guy who gave you a lift? She asked. Turns out he wrote the sleaze columns. Heck, what did I say! Thankfully no mention of yours truly. He obviously didn't consider my life sleazy enough!

Rock-and-Roll, cigarettes and booze

Living in Victoria and at home on holiday, I went to a local dance and met a naval officer. A great dancer! By coincidence, his sister also lived in Tachbrook St. He said he would be at sea for the next nine months but asked if he could phone me on his return to take me out. Almost nine months to the day he did and we arranged to go dancing at the Lyceum Ballroom.

Just so happened that a rock-and-roll competition was due to take place. We entered. Soon dozens of couples were whittled down to two. First prize was a trip to Japan to take part in the finals. We, as runners up, received umpteen packets of cigarettes and bottles of Scotch. I didn't drink or smoke in those days so my partner got the lot! Still, it had all been great fun!

He also sailed off into the sunset!

Party hardy

I held lots of parties at our large flat in Earls Court Road, which I shared with Norma and four other girls. A tall Irish man asked to use the phone. Some weeks later we received an astronomical phone bill. On checking I notice a long-distance call to Ireland. Aha and then I remembered!

One day said Irish man appears, full of apologies and said that his mate had told him that he had been a bit pissed, gate-crashed my party and made a long call to his mum in Ireland on her birthday. He had come to pay for the call. Such honesty in the middle of London!

Short S(c)hrift for Bud

At another of our parties I met a South African, Bud (Richard) a racing driver from Durban. His car, a Dart, wasn't competitive in the UK so he became a mechanic for Stirling Moss, along with his brother Eddie and another South African, Pete. He used to drive me around in a limo with Stirling Moss Automobile Association emblazoned on the side. I felt like the bee's knees!

He used to take me to see the races at Brands Hatch, get me into the Pits and let me time the laps. A press photographer took a pic of me draped over the Lola Chev (or Big Banger as it was known). At the post match braai* I met many of the famous racing drivers. Jim Clark, Graham Hill, Bruce McLaren et al.

One evening before going out Bud, being very conscientious, decided to first check on the cars. Approaching the garage, he motioned me to shh as he could hear noises. Creeping in he finds the night watchman fast asleep, snoring his head off and his radio blaring. Bud thought they were being burgled!

On another occasion, he and Pete were tasked with babysitting Stirling's Mayfair apartment while he and his wife were on holiday. Pete, being a real naughty dude, began pressing all the buttons on the headboard at the back of the bed. Soon water was gushing down the stairs. By remote control he'd turned on all the bathroom taps...the First Great Flood Disaster!

Luckily, I wasn't around to help them mop up! One of Bud's quirks, he hated alarm clocks so one evening I sneaked one under his pillow, set for 4am. I wish you could have seen the state of the clock once he'd hurled it against the wall!

On a trip to the States where he was putting the car through some races, he proposed by letter (whatever happened to the down on one knee bit?) but I was still nursing a broken heart, my Irish man having returned to Joburg so another romance petered out! I did hear that he went on to marry some Polish Countess, so I guess that makes him Count Bud!!

*South Africa; Grill (meat) over an open fire.

Spanish vegetables

Still living in my large Earls Court flat, Paula, one of the flatmates, and I had booked a holiday in Campello, near Benidorm. We stayed in Casa; the only accommodation available in Campello. An offbeat boarding house on the beach, it was run by a Kiwi, South African from Pretoria and an Englishman. We were given a bed and blanket, use of a communal kitchen and all cutlery, crockery and pots and pans were supplied.

The guys would go fishing and the girls cooked the meals. On the beach I met Juanita, girlfriend of the Englishman. Being half gypsy, music and dancing were in her blood. She had two American friends, one black, one white, who had left the States some years before and never returned. They both played Spanish guitar.

One evening she invited me to their apartment in Alicante. Flimsy curtains wafting in the breeze, lights dimmed, Juanita, barefooted and clad in gypsy dress, danced to their beautiful guitar music. My favourite was Romance Anonymo, so called because the composer was unknown. So haunting, it brought tears to my eyes! Her boyfriend, disapproving of her American friends, kept her on a tight leash, getting her home undetected was a bit cloak and dagger, as she was sure she was being followed but it had been a magical evening. You couldn't PAY for entertainment like this!

Sitting by the roadside early on the morning of our departure, Paula and I were trying to hitch a lift. Eventually, a vegetable lorry lumbered up. Paula sat in the cab beside the driver whilst I perched precariously atop the veggies, not the most comfortable of rides but we made our Barcelona train on time. It had been a great holiday and a very cheap one!

The movie that never was

My last residence before emigrating was in Earls Court Road but in order to fully appreciate this story, it's important to get the geography right. On ground level was a tobacconist, atop The Vegetarian Restaurant and above that our cute but miniscule attic flat. The restaurant was owned and catered by a very elegant, Oxford educated divorced Irish man named Mr W-P.

One night, Norma (she of the floating chiffon) and I were awaiting our beaux to take us to dinner. They duly arrived on time. All duckied up, I was ready but Norma was still washing her hair. She joined us looking very sexy in swathed turban and for half an hour we solved the political woes of the nation.

"OMG" shouts Norma making beeline for the bathroom. It turns out she'd left the taps running and the place was flooded! After bailing that lot out, another OMG moment. "The restaurant" we screamed! Stripping down to their jocks and we in shorts and tops, we bolted downstairs to find the place swimming in water!

Well, after bailing this lot out and sticking sacks of potatoes, carrots and onions in the three industrial gas ovens, at 3am we declared "he'll never know!" But just in case, we'd better have a good story ready. Now Mr W-P, it's about your ridiculously small sink!

As luck would have it, Norma bangs straight into said gent. "Now Mr W-P, it's.." but before she could finish her spiel, he says "Now Norma, don't look at me with those big brown eyes, I know my restaurant has never been as clean, I can write off a few mouldy sacks of soggy veggies and I dare say the astronomical gas bill won't break the bank, but go downstairs to Mr Tobacconist and explain away his hundreds of pounds worth of soggy cigarette stocks!"

Quite! Later that night as we were packing for Pitcairn, a gentle knock on the door and in walks Mr W-P. "Now, now, ladies, no need to do anything hasty, but pleeeeze don't let it happen again!"

There was a sorry sequel to that story. Years later, living in SA and on holiday in Scotland, I decided to spend last few days in London, looking up old friends. On arriving at Earls Court Road, to my dismay I found restaurant all boarded up and no indication as to where Mr W-P had gone. I casually strolled into Mr Tobacconist to enquire but the glare from his gimlet eye stopped me mid track.

After all these years he hadn't forgotten me, so I turned tail and made a hasty exit!

Restaurant Operetta

One Sunday morning we hear the most beautiful singing from downstairs. Peering over the balcony, we see this apparition, bum in air, doek* on head, rubber gloves up to her elbows, on her knees, scrubbing the floor and singing her heart out. "Your char has the most beautiful voice" we told Mr W-P later.

"Char, CHAR!" he spluttered, "that 'char', as you so delicately put it, just happens to be one of Covent Garden's most supreme opera singers!" Then why is she scrubbing floors? "Oh, she finds it therapeutic". Turns out she was his girlfriend! He took us into his office and showed us his photos albums, full of pictures of said 'char 'decked out in all her finery, performing at Covent Garden.

* a square of cloth worn mainly by African women to cover the head, from Afrikaans: cloth

Part 3: Tata to London, hello Johannesburg

I emigrated to South Africa in December 1966. I had received promotion to a higher grade but the posting took so long to come through that by then I had completed my arrangements to emigrate. Setting sail from Southampton on the Pendennis Castle, the trip took three weeks.

I won the fancy dress competition, my theme being Topic of Cancer. All costumes had to be spontaneous and prepared on board. My top and slacks were covered in empty cigarette boxes collected for me by the waiters. I borrowed a small trolley on wheels from the kid's play-room, attached a broom handle, tied a balloon with Topic of Cancer painted on it. Next, I dunked my face in a bag of flour and painted black circles under my eyes.

I asked a waiter to unlock my trunk in the hold and fetch me a long strip of linen covered in book matches (one of my hobbies in London) and a lampshade made out of cig-arette packets. This had been made for me by a disabled man in thanks for finding him a job.

Borrowing the captain's pipe, and with a cigar and cig-arettes dangling from my lips and fingers, I steered my lit-tle ship across the deck expecting at any moment to land in the laps of the judges, there being quite a bit of turbu-lence at the time!

I witnessed the exciting spectacle of a stowaway being transferred from the Pendennis to the Windsor Castle go-ing in the opposite direction. The daft bat had sent his clothes to the laundry with his cabin number on it!

Pied Piper of Canines

I initially stayed with Paula who had emigrated to Joburg the year before I, at a Berea boarding house named The Odyssey. I eventually secured more suitable accommodation in a commune in Park Town West. I had my own flat let and there were five other tenants.

My landlady was a very wealthy Jewish widow who owned several other houses in the area. A bit of a snoop, she was always poking around the house while we were at work, so I acquired a beautiful Alsatian named Rhea. A neighbour reported that one day Rhea had her pinned against the front wall for hours until he rescued her! She obviously didn't trust her one bit and proved to be an excellent guard. I used to put her on her leash when I returned from work and take her for walks round the block.

One day we were joined by Fred Basset from next door and soon after by Rotti, a big black ugly Rottweiler. I would often hear his owner groan oh no, not again each time he surveyed the wreckage of his newly repaired fence! Two Scotties from across the road joined in and before long I had a motley assortment of breeds, all following obediently one behind the other in strict formation.

Up Loch Avenue to Jan Smuts, wait for the lights to change at the robots, cross over, down the other side and along another street. I felt like the Pied Piper of Park Town!! Bemused bus passengers going along Jan Smuts must have thought I was Barbara Woodhouse doing dog training!

Lock-Up

I was employed as Personal Officer of The Belfast department store in Market Street. My office was in the corner of Soft Furnishings. One evening working late and unaware of the time, I opened my door to find the place deserted and everyone gone home.

I was securely locked in! What to do! I did consider snuggling down under the duvet of one of the beds but thought I'd better make an attempt to get out. Now it takes three keyholders to open the store. By the time I phoned them, one was on the train going home, one was at the movies with his wife and the third in the pub down the road.

They eventually arrived to let me out, furious at having their evening ruined! Bemused passers-by must have thought they had witnessed a robbery in progress!

Kurt and Val in Vogue

A friend of mine had recovered from a slipped disc op. She gave me her board which I stowed behind my kitchen door. My boyfriend at the time, a very talented German artist / photographer was Display manager of the Belfast. His name was Kurt. He said he would make me a coffee table out of it as soon as he had time.

One day I noticed it was missing. No need to wonder who had taken it. I phoned Mrs G and demanded my board back. "Valerie darlink, go down to Greenside and take any wood that you vant." "I don't want your rotten old wood; I want my board back." It was not forthcoming. I penned her a note, dear Mrs G, herewith my check for my month's rental, less R 200 for the board and R100 for the inconvenience. She never said another word!

She used to drive around in a rattletrap of a van. I never understood why as she could have afforded a Ferrari! One day she said I must come to her house on the other side of Jan Smuts to view her latest DIY efforts. Her boudoir she had decked out in garish purple, satin bedcovers and incense burning everywhere! It looked like a Chinese brothel, truly awful!

Kurt took me camping to Durban but somewhere he took a wrong turning and ended up halfway back to Joburg. By the time we arrived in Durban it was very late so we pitched tent on the first available piece of beach we could find. Early next morning we were awakened by the lifeguards telling us to move as we were parked outside their hut!

On another occasion he took me camping to Lourenco Marques but working late it was again very late when we arrived and visibility was poor. Kurt parked on the nearest piece of open ground he could find.

Early next morning we were awakened by the hooting of car horns. We were parked in the car park of the Polana Hotel! That wouldn't have been so bad but I had dossed down in my sleeping bag at the side of the car. I must have looked quite a sight!

Being bored with retail I obtained employment as Personnel Officer with an engineering company in Selby,

National Trading. Kurt won many awards and trophies with his displays at the Rand Easter Show using machines from our woodworking division. I was flattered to find he named his business Vogue Graphics after my initials!

Hund vergessen

One day Mrs G gathered us together and said proposals were afoot to build the M6 motorway running through Park Town West and she would eventually have to give us notice. A girlfriend Lee, asked me to join her large flat in Bellview. Not knowing what the future would hold I jumped at the opportunity.

My boyfriend at the time, Ian, an architect from Glasgow, helped me do a midnight flit with the aid of his truck. I took everything except the curtains, hoping to avoid detection for as long as possible. Next morning, I get a phone call at work. "Valerie darlink, you have gone but that flipping Hund is still here!"

I obviously couldn't take Rhea to a flat so Mary, one of the tenants who was moving to a house in Empire Road, offered to take her. Ian was living in a Houghton commune called The Circus, with five other Scots.

And a circus it truly was, with a pub in the basement, raucous parties with discos, fancy dress and fondue evenings. It was a real swinging pad!

Mauritius

One year I went solo on holiday to Mauritius. On the plane I befriended tall blonde Gayle. Working for American Express, she had been tasked with checking out the state of the various hotels and reporting back to her office in Joburg. She was given free use of a small jeep for a week and in no time, we had explored the whole island.

Sitting on the veranda having a drink the evening of our arrival, two Mauritians drove past in a 4 / 4 and asked us if we would care to go for a drive up the mountain to view a stag farm. Our lovely hotel, The Morne Plage was situated on the beach at the Base of the mountain.

One of the chaps, Patrick, was the son of the director of New Mauritius Hotels and he owned a stag farm halfway up the mountain. Opening the gates, we were confronted by a magnificent sight. Hundreds of pairs of eyes shining in the darkness, truly spectacular!

They became our unofficial tour guides for the duration of our stay. They took us out in their glass bottomed boat, on pedallos, snorkelling, fishing and trips to isolated beaches. Here they started to show off, diving and doing summersaults from a dizzy height off the rocks into the sea below. They should be in the Olympics I thought but didn't say so. Just sat primly on the beach dipping my toes in the water and saying your nuts!

One afternoon on the beach a good-looking Mauritian invited me to a casino some distance from the hotel. He owned his own yacht. After losing most of my money at the casino, we went to a bar for a drink. There he promptly announced that he didn't feel like driving all the way back to my hotel and I could stay with him at his apartment. Not blerry likely I thought, I hardly know you and told him to bugger off!

Looking in my handbag I notice that I still had his cheque book which he'd given me for safekeeping but no money for a B and B, or even a taxi back. What to do! A very nice English lady, noticing my distress, asked me what the problem was.

Consider yourself lucky, that guy is a renowned play-boy and a real cad! She introduced me to a Spanish friend who said he'd give me a lift back. By the time we arrived it was very late and he said he would sleep in his car. Well, I have a spare bed in my room which you can have if you behave yourself, which he did..a perfect gentleman!

Next day playboy sailed past in his yacht and I took great delight in tearing his check book to shreds and throwing them into the sea! I note to self: when on holiday, do NOT get picked up by good-looking males with yachts! Gayle, meanwhile, had befriended the chap who organised all the sports activities and equipment. He had at cute little cottage deep in the forest.

Many happy hours were spent there, he playing his gui-tar and we singing along. We were there in the early hours on the morning of our departure. How we made the plane I'll never know! But it had been another great holiday!

Zdravo Vic

Lee and I eventually moved to an apartment in Majestic Towers on the corner of Clarendon Circle. An elegant building, it was the scene of one of the James Bond movies. Early on the morning of New Year's Day, wee Bob, one of the Circus inmates, came rapping on my window.

He was hosting a New Year's Day lunch at the Norwood home of a friend and wanted to invite me along. Having just returned from a New Year's Eve party at few hours before, I was whacked! "Only thirty people and you will know everyone." So, I reluctantly agreed to go. Wee Bob asked me to check on a guy sitting alone outside on the veranda. "Ask him to join the party." So, going up to him I asked him why he was being so anti-social. "Well, I don't know anybody", obviously a bit shy.

And so, it was that one year later, in 1974, Vic, a Serbian from Belgrade, and I were married in a quaint old church in Braamfontein, acquiring the unwieldy surname of Miličević. He goes around telling everyone I picked him up!

We honeymooned in the Seychelles. At a hotel dance one night, who should appear but my Irish man with an Emirates hostess on his arm (he always had some doll on his arm!) We passed each other in the aisle of the plane going home but didn't speak. And that's the last I saw of him.

But imagine, a chap I met ten years before in London, should rock up on my honeymoon in the Seychelles!

What are the chances! 85 years now and a confirmed bachelor, he lives in the Southern suburbs in a house he had built to his own design.

Stefan

Vic and I lived initially in a top floor apartment of Majestic Towers. We soon moved to a Rosettenville semi owned by his parents, they living in the semi next door. Our son Stefan was born 9 months later.

One day I took him in his stroller to the local shops where I had espied a certain item in a boutique window which I fancied. I told him that if he was a good boy, I would buy him an ice cream. He was with me in the changeroom, at the till, but when I went to exit, poof, no Stefan!

In the blink of an eye, he had done a Houdini on me! Panic stations as everyone started searching for him. I even dashed down to Woollies on the corner and asked them to page his description over the loud speaker, to no avail. A thorough search of the very busy car park brought no result.

Going back to the boutique, I noticed a waiter standing outside a cafe, looking up and down the street. Approaching him he said "Ma'am have you lost your son?" Whew! There was Stef sitting quietly at a table without a care in the world. "I offered him a cool drink and something to eat but he said no, his mum had said if he was a good boy, she'd buy him an ice cream."

I had visions of having to take him back to Soweto! "But why did you come to this particular café?" I asked. "Because you had taken me here before." I couldn't remember that!

The time came to enter high school. I took him for an interview with the principal of Parktown Boys. "What do you like to read he asked?" "Comics" said Stef. Well, I wanted the ground to open up and swallow me! "Oh, do you, I love comics myself." I then took him for an interview with Greenside High. He was accepted by both schools. "Which one do you prefer?" "Greenside." "Why?" "Because they've got girls there!" That's my boy!

He matriculated and did his B Com by correspondence through Unisa. Being an avid cricket fan, he had a part time job as cricket statistician at the Wanderers. He also wrote cricket columns for the sports column of the Star newspaper.

One year he went on holiday to Ireland and my dear Irish friend, Jacinta, being a bit of a matchmaker, introduced him to Louise. He returned but wasn't a happy chappie! Aged 28 he flew the coop and returned to Ireland, a painful parting but inevitable. They married and live in Co. Kildare with my three beautiful granddaughters.

Extended Holiday

At aged 60, on holiday solo in Scotland, I fell out of bed, it being much narrower than my king size in Joburg, hitting my head on the brass table lamp. This resulted in a detached retina requiring an emergency operation at the

Princess Alexandra eye hospital in Edinburgh. The operation was a success and I was hospitalized for three days.

After my operation I was sitting in the lounge where two Scots from up north were helping me locate the cricket channel on tv. I must have been the only patient remotely interested in cricket! Matron comes in and asks if we'd like coffee. "Yes please!" "And toast?" "Oh yes please!" Freshly percolated coffee and stacks of golden toast dripping with butter, it was DIVINE!

I had made friends with a rather quaint little Scot, tattoos all over, with a cap perched on his head covered in badges he had collected on his travels around the globe. He was in for a cornea transplant. "Fancy a fish supper hen?" "And how pray are you going to get that?" Taking me to the window he said "See that car over there? Well, it's mine and I'll be back in a bit."

He returned soon after with fish and chips wrapped in newspaper and dripping with vinegar...scrumptious! "Fancy a wee puff?" Did I ever! "But you can't smoke in here!" "Go to the ladies, climb up on the stool, hang out the window and you can puff away to your heart's content." How did he know that I wondered! "But come outside and we can have a fag."

Jimmying the door so as we as could get back in, he proudly showed me his stack of stompies beneath the window. As we were puffing away, an elegant gentleman approached him and began chatting. "Who was that?" I asked. "Oh, he is my anaesthetist" he said airily.

It struck me as hilarious that he was blowing smoke into the face of his anaesthetist! A gas bubble had been inserted behind my eye to keep my eyeball in place. It had to disperse before I could fly home so my month's holiday turned into six weeks.

Stef phoned me to say they had got something I always wanted, security gates all-round the house. I should have smelled a rat! Vic met me at OR Tambo. "We have good news and bad news." "I'll take the bad news." "Well, we've had a burglary but the good news is nothing much was taken." Ah that explains the security gates. Bit late I thought now that the horse has bolted!

Arriving home, I opened my wardrobe, the lock of which had been forced, to find all my jewellery missing. The only other things taken were Vic's spare car keys and all the meat from the freezer.

Now almost 82 years, almost crippled with arthritis of the knees, I ponder why, after having led such an energetic and eventful life, it has come to this. But that's life, I guess. No-one goes unscathed through the passage of time!

THE END

With grateful thanks to my dear friend and confidante, Jacinta Wagner of Munich, for her hard work and enthusiasm in the compilation of these memoirs.

List of Illustrations

The author

Ivor

General Franco´s rear end, Palma de Mallorca

Hitching a lift, Casa Campello

Holland Rd. Miss S hosting a Christmas Day lunch for her tenants

Brands Hatch with Lola Chev

Norma in Edinburgh

Fancy dress aboard Pendennis Castle

Transfer of stowaway to Windsor Castle

Parktown West commune

Majestic Towers

Wedding Day

On honeymoon in Seychelles

Zeitfracht Medien GmbH
Ferdinand-Jühlke-Straße 7
99095 Erfurt, Deutschland
produktsicherheit@kolibri360.de